LOVE ON GREENER PASTURES

A NOVELETTE

BRITT JONI

B. LOVE PUBLICATIONS

INTRODUCTION

Note: This is a novelette. If you are looking for something full length please try one of my other titles. It's a quick read. 7 chapters of love. This novelette serves as a healing point. It's tying my past to my present. It's full of love. It's full of healing. It's really just a sweet way to show you who Britt Joni is and what she represents. This is where love meets the soul and also where love HEALS the soul. Please enjoy this sweet introduction of what's soon to come.

Peace, Blessings, & Positive vibes,

Britt

Check out the playlist:

Spotify: http://bit.ly/LOGPspotify

Apple Music: https://apple.co/2u7xd5A

Love on Greener Pastures
PLAYLIST

Grass ain't greener	Chris Brown
Cranes in the sky	Solange
Breakeven	The Script
Surprise me	Mahalia
I remember	Mahalia
Faded Pictures	Case & Joe
Sweet love	Anita Baker
On Chill	Wale & Jeremih
Wicked Games	Kiana Ledé
I want you around	Snoh Aalegra
Soul Inspiration	Anita Baker
Exit Wounds	Luke James
Sorry	6lack
Best of me	Anthony Hamilton
Show me love	Alicia Keys & Miguel
Hard Place	H.E.R.

Britt Joni

sla

OUT OF ALL THE nights for me to be left alone, drowning in my own thoughts, tonight would be the night that everyone let me sulk in peace. New Year's Eve. While everyone else was out celebrating, making love, and just enjoying all that love could be, I was drowning in regret. I was once them, but I foolishly let the man that I knew I needed get away by not nurturing my fruit once I saw it bud.

I was too busy chasing a dream. A dream of a perfect man, one who provided all of the things I needed financially. While I had all of the things I needed materialistically, my heart and soul were in some serious debt. My grown ass thought I had what I needed, but that was not the case. I was foolish in chasing what was right.

If I'm being real, that dream was securing my future, or so I thought, but in no way was it worth me losing my heart. Tennyson was like cool summer rain on a beautiful Sunday morning. Refreshing, warm, and easy going. His stormy, gray eyes and tapered, wooly beard plastered against his milk chocolate skin would make the hardest sinner turned saint, just to be in the presence of perfection. He was my everything, and nothing short of my muse for the paintings and portraits I created. What most didn't realize is that all of my art pieces told a story of how I once had a love so deep that I worshiped heaven and earth to keep it. I found it so deeply rooted in Jerusalem that I kept a cup for Jesus on my nightstand.

So, how did I get here you may ask? Pride, greed, and a stubborn heart. My ringing phone brought me out of my thoughts. Seeing that it was a person I was currently ignoring, my chill mood instantly changed. Life sure had a way of humbling you. The devil presented me with a beautifully wrapped package of everything I thought I wanted, and during the morning time when my flesh was at its weakest, I jumped at that opportunity. Regardless of who it hurt, I jumped at it. I went from being secure in my relationship to questioning it at every bend of the road. I wasn't foolish, I knew that with success stress surely would come. I just didn't think that stress would result in me being home all alone on a holiday.

"What do you want, Ryder?" I asked, answering the phone with so much attitude that I knew Satan was doing a little jig.

"Isla, why must you be this way every time I call you? It's not becoming of a woman to be the way that you are when you have a man laying all that you desire at your footstep. You knew the ramifications of being with a successful man. Baby, I'm rare!" Ryder stated.

"Ryder, you're not that damn rare, so let's just stop it there. I understand that you are busy, but I hardly see you.

If we are being real here, I never see you— only in passing, and I'm just not okay with that. At this point, I need more and I'm tired of the repetitive conversations about it. If I wanted to be lonely, I could do just that and be just that— alone," I declared.

"I mean, what did you expect? Did you expect me to sit around and stare at your ass all day, like Tennyson?" As he yelled, "No, I'm not that nigga, baby," I heard a woman giggle in the background. I just knew like hell his ass wasn't out getting his dick wet while I was sitting at home.

"I know I didn't just hear a bitch in the background when yo' ass is supposed to be working? See, what you're not gonna do is have me sitting at home like some wack ass bitch while you are out doing what the fuck you want to do. I'm not the one or the two! Where the fuck are you at!"

"I'm at work, where else would I be?" Ryder confirmed. "The bitch you hear is my secretary! Stop being so damn insecure." He moaned out, "I'm all about you."

"See, I know yo' ass didn't just call me while you fucking another bitch!" I spat out. "You, for real, got me all types of fucked up. Since you out doing you, remember not to shit bricks once you catch me doing me!" I disconnected the call.

If I was lucky, I could make it down to Kituko Nyeusi before they closed. I wish I would sit around pouting when I could be at the club making my ass jump with my girls.

Fuck Ryder!

ennyson

WHEN ISLA LEFT me for Ryder, initially, I was hurt, but I understood her plight. We were at a point where we needed to grow, and bills needed to be paid. Yes, we loved each other, but love wasn't going to pay our bills. She wasn't with struggle love and as selfish as it was I respected it. She wasn't built like I was but I loved her anyway. I just wished now that she saw Ryder wasn't shit, that love would be enough to bring her back. Yes, he was successful in his own right, but in no way did that make it ok that he was cheating on my girl.

The blogs always had him on their websites for one reason or another, but nothing made my skin boil more than watching the man that she left me for getting his dick sucked in the middle of the club by some random ass groupie. I honestly wanted to put his head through a wall, but that wasn't my place. She made her choice and unfortunately, this time, I couldn't protect her heart. She had to deal with the reality that her inability to stick things out was the reason why she could no longer count on my love. I couldn't continue to hurt myself to fix her. All she had to do was remain patient and we would've been great. But no, she was too consumed with looking at the green grass on the other side of the fence that she neglected to water her own.

So, I was cool on that.

"Tennyson, we are low on Hennessy. Can you go grab some more? You know how niggas start acting when we run out. Last time, they almost tore yo' shit down," my bartender, Rio, called out.

Before I could get down the hall to my office, I caught a whiff of a fragrance I hadn't smelled in forever. The scent was familiar. It was nostalgic. It brought back painful memories and a ton of grief. But it just couldn't be whom I thought it was. She had long moved on and forgotten about the two of us. There was no purpose in her coming into my space. Why would she show up here? Why now?

"Tennyson, baby, can we talk?" I heard her angelic voice call out, and I would be lying if I said the shit didn't make me feel some type of way. I instantly froze because there was no way she was back. The universe wouldn't be this cruel to me. I was still nursing the wounds of our past. So there was no way that she was here in my space wanting to talk to me. I shook my head and blinked three times and sure enough she was still there smiling timidly.

"Yeah, Doll. Follow me into my office," I said, trying to mask my emotions from her. Once we were inside the privacy of my office I closed the door and really took her in. Nothing has changed about her. She looked so angelic but I could tell there was some heaviness surrounding her. That heaviness was what had her heading back to me. Her pride was telling her I was her safe bet but no longer was I going to be the person she ran to when she messed things up in her life. I wasn't her fall guy. "So tell me, what brings you here after all these years?"

"I wanted to clear the air."

"Isla, you're a smart woman and I'd like to think that I'm a very intelligent man. So I would appreciate it if you stop playing with my intelligence and let me know what it is that you want."

"Okay, since you want honesty. Simply put, I want you."

"That can't happen. In fact, in this space that I'm in right now, I'm more than certain it won't happen."

"And why not?"

"I don't want it to happen. I'm not your healing post."

"Tennyson that was years ago. We were kids. I'm a better person now."

"Kids huh? My wounds are still fresh. Just because you're over it doesn't mean that I am."

"I know I was wrong, but it was before I truly knew the depth of what I mean to you. I feared losing you, losing control, but I'm yours, baby. Completely yours," she pleaded.

"Isla, I can't in good faith go down this road with you again. You really hurt me, Doll."

"Baby, I want to give you the love you deserve. I saw the error of my ways. I see the God in you, and all my fears fall aside. That's what makes me love you. I made the conscious decision to rise in love with you because I refused to fall.

"Falling is the equivalent of failing, and that's just something I didn't see for us. You may not see it and you may not feel it, but baby, I'm telling you. I love you for the both of us, and I'll be damned if I lose you now. I'm not beneath begging, but don't make me beg baby," she pleaded while grabbing me by my waist, pulling me close.

"No. Just no," I said while pushing her away. "I need time. If you care anything about me, just give me that."

After she took a moment to see if what I was saying was reflecting in my eyes, her tears started to fall. As if it clicked that I couldn't overcome the hurt she had caused when she walked out of my studio apartment that day, she kissed my lips and walked out of my office.

No matter how bad I wanted her to come back and fight, no matter how urgent I felt the need was to run after her, I knew that I couldn't. Yes, people make mistakes, but giving someone who was capable of damaging your heart the opportunity to do so again was downright foolish. So, no. She had to go.

There had to be action in what you said. I had to feel your love and, ultimately, I didn't feel it with her. So, as much as it hurt to watch her walk away, I had to let her. If nothing else, for the sake of preserving everything that was great within me, she had to go. She had to accept that the grass is never greener on the other side, and if it was, it was lined with bullshit.

As soon as the coast was clear, I sat down at my desk and ran my fingers across a tattered picture of the two of us. Back when times were simpler, when all it took to make her smile was an impromptu walk to the park overlooking the river, or surprising her with paint or binge-watching art documentaries on Netflix and Hulu.

Feeling the hurt starting to sink in from dredging up our past and trying to figure out where everything went wrong, I took that tattered picture and threw it against the wall. I don't even know why I allowed her in my space to speak. It was clear that she clearly didn't understand my love for her.

I wanted her, but I couldn't fathom allowing her to continue on with me like everything could go back to normal, because it couldn't. She hurt me. Hell, if I'm being completely honest, baby girl gutted me and left me broken. It took a lot to put me back together, and I'd be damned if I gave her that opportunity to break me down again. I deserved better than to get a love that could easily be pushed aside.

I knew at this point, with the hurt sinking in deep, I was no good for my bar. I quickly refilled the bar and made my way home. It was just like her to waltz back into my life, fuck shit up, and leave me with the disgusting feeling of regret and the stench of fear. As I lay in my bed, overlooking the beautiful fireworks lighting up the city, I said a quick prayer asking God to deliver and release me from my personal prison. At the stroke of midnight, I finally gave in and

cried over a love lost.

sla

How COULD I have been so stupid? I poured my heart out to Tennyson, along with my regrets of walking away. Yet, he wasn't willing to see past his hurt. We were good together. Damn near perfect. The only blemish we'd ever had was me not being able to wait it out for him. He may say he can't have me in his life now, but he will see that with me was where he needed to be.

As I made my way through the crowded bar, I couldn't get rid of the sour taste of defeat in my mouth. I wanted to go back to his office and plead some more but what good would that do when he stood firm in everything he said to me. I caused this, but I felt deep in my soul that he could've at least given us another shot. No, things didn't have to always work when I was ready for them to work, but he for damn sure could've met me halfway. He loved me, I saw it in his eyes that he did. He was just too damned stubborn to admit it, but at this point, I showed my hands; it was now on him to come back to me.

I got back into my car and raced over to Ryder's. I needed to dead this whole thing once and for all. I'd been a fool for lesser things, but I would be damned if I allowed Ryder to continue to make a fool out of me like I was some wack bitch. Nah, he'd played me long enough. It was high time that I recognized my own worth and corrected the mistake that I made. If I couldn't have Tennyson then I was for damn sure done wasting my energy on Ryder. I was going back to my holistic roots and purging everything I thought I needed from the soul out.

My thoughts were halted by the vehicle parked in his driveway. This just couldn't be! This was like a gut punch, sucking all the life out of me. I swear, no matter how bad a person is, no one— and I mean absolutely no one— deserved this. I whipped my matte black Camaro SS into his drive-way, blocking both cars. Regardless of what I lacked in the department of love for him, I could never wrap my head around this form of betrayal.

As I stepped out of the vehicle, I threw on a pair of sweats and sneakers I had stuck in my trunk. I couldn't help but to chuckle at the fact that my scattered brain and my onset spout of laziness in cleaning out my car had now come in handy. Funny enough, it was Ryder who said nothing would come from my messiness. Soon, he would realize it had me more than a little bit prepared for what would surely be the grand finale of us.

We weren't supposed to be together. That fact was made evident in the amount of time I spent lusting and longing for another man, but I never once disrespected Ryder. Like a fool, I rode the wave of our love affair with no remorse or regards to the outside world. I kept riding because superficially, on paper, we were perfect for one another. We were safe for each other from the outside looking in. We were okay living this lie, until the pain of what should've never been suffocated me. It was like I was drowning in this cesspool of dysfunction, but instead of my lungs filling themselves with water, it was disgust and resentment causing my soul to sink and be anchored in an abyss of darkness.

As I crept into the home of the man I thought would love me and provide a stable lifestyle for me, I was caught off guard as I felt the tears flow down my face. I wasn't sure if it was his betrayal of my heart that stung, or if it was the fact that Tennyson wanted nothing to do with me. I knew there was no turning back now. I had to see this through and, after I hurt for a bit, I would pull myself together so that I could never fall into this sunken place again.

Making my way down the darkened hallway, I was greeted with a smell of musk, sweet perfume and, unfortunately, sex. My heart began pounding like it wanted to pop right out of my chest, and my body was flushed with a heat that would rival Satan's lair.

"Ah shit! Right there, Daddy!" The voice sliced my ear drums like a rusty razor blade.

"Shut the fuck up and take this dick, Jessica!" Ryder's stupid ass moaned out as he continued to drill her out. The passion I saw in his face pushed me further over the edge. How can this nigga proclaim so much love for me, but continue to fuck other bitches? It was exasperating to think of the many times he held me in his arms and made me think it was all in my damn head. He did this, knowing full well he was fucking someone close to me.

I stood there and watched them like a psycho voyeur, so that it was embedded into my skull. I needed these scenes to replay as a constant reminder of why I would never trust or forgive either of them. Feeling I'd seen enough under what would have normally been a beautiful full moon, I walked over to the bedside table, picked up his celebratory blunt, and sparked up.

"What the fuck!" Ryder yelled as he struggled to cut the lights on. Bitch should've known he was using her body as a cum bucket when he wouldn't even fuck her with the lights on. But, being that they were spending NYE together, maybe it was I who meant nothing.

"Oh shit, sis! This is not what it looks like. I can explain!" Jessica exclaimed as she saw my tear-stained face. She hurriedly jumped her nasty ass into her clothes as I filled my lungs with the thick smoke of Kush.

"So, you're telling me I didn't just see my nigga balls deep in your guts, *sis*?" I snarled out as I ashed the blunt.

"Baby, please let me explain," Ryder requested while trying to pull me into a hug. I muffed the shit out of him because he had me fucked up in three different ways. His ass was not only cheating on me, but he was cheating on me with my best damn friend. Then, he had the audacity to try to rub up on me, with his nasty ass body. Not only did he have sex with her, he didn't have the common courtesy to stand clear until he washed the smell of her off. After glancing around more, I saw that these bitches had failed to utilize a condom. At that moment, I felt sick. I was more than done with them both.

"There is nothing to explain here, just know that I am done! And, as for you, bitch." I turned around swiftly and punched her right in between the eyes. "Stay the fuck away from me because the next time, I'm liable to shoot yo' snake ass!"

As I turned to make my exit, I made myself a vow to be

a better me for me. I had to realize no one in this world owed me anything. They didn't have to give me the courtesy of respecting me because it wasn't their duty to do so when I wasn't demanding it. I never realized what a grave mistake that was, until tonight. I allowed people to give me half of what I was worth and I foolishly accepted it because in my mind something was better than nothing. Boy was I wrong on so many levels. I deserved better from not only other people, but me as well. After I pulled myself out of this slump, I knew for a fact that I would never put myself in a situation where I was destined to fail. I was going to protect my heart and my happiness at all costs.

By the time I made it to my home, I was defeated and completely numb to all emotions. I took a quick shower, moisturized my body, slipped into my silk pajamas, and placed a bonnet on my head. As the clock struck midnight, I looked at myself in the mirror and whispered out, "Happy New Year," while vowing to make a change.

The next morning, I woke up to seventy-seven missed calls and an equal amount of texts but I was drained. I wasn't going down that road with Ryder again. It was time to change how I dealt with things. It was time for me to purge all of the feelings that made me feel like I needed him. It was high time for me to stop thinking I needed any man to make me whole or to make me happy. Tennyson included.

No longer was I going to operate in survival mode, I was going to truly heal. After blocking Ryder from all avenues of my life I pulled out my singing bowl. I needed to feel centered, to find some peace and have a clear head before I made my next move.

I spent a solid hour meditating and though I felt lighter I still felt a heaviness seeping through. It was there, and I knew if I didn't address it now I would forever go through life repeating the same patterns until I fully learned life's lessons. I turned on my favorite mindfulness guru Maverick Cooper beautifully spoken affirmations of healing before I sat down to soak in my spiritual bath. His words coated me and gave me all of the strength that I could muster up in this moment.

With tears rolling down my face I knew then that I needed help. I knew then that I was going to have to put in some long hours but I also knew that I was going to need a therapist to help me purge, grieve, and heal. So as I sank and soaked I made a mental checklist to call up a therapy office that dealt with past traumas and schedule an appointment. I also vowed that as I washed away the remnants of last night and let them flow down the drain that I couldn't carry that weight into the next phase of my life. It was high time I truly heal.

CHAPTER 4

ennyson

SIX MONTHS LATER....

Business had been great for me lately, but my personal affairs were suffering. I couldn't date because my heart wasn't settled. The day I allowed my pride to dominate my heart was the catalyst in the slump I felt myself in. Nothing and no one around me could bring me peace. I don't know how many times my pride had stopped me from beating down my love's door. I needed her like I needed my next breath, but I couldn't trust her with my heart.

So, I filled my time making my business great. I didn't know much, but I knew my business would never break my heart. Hence, me sitting in this crowded restaurant going over business plans to make my second location a successful venture. This had to be a success since nothing else in my personal life was working. The only love I needed in my life was money, since the woman I loved cut me deep.

The moment the energy changed in this restaurant, I knew it had to be my sweet, stubborn Isla. Her energy was potent. It was like a soft summer breeze begging to be seen and absorbed. The sweet smell of her perfume was tickling my nose as the melody of her genuine laughter was making love to my ears. As I glanced over at her table, I felt a burning sensation in the pit of my stomach. There was no way this woman was as happy and free as she was letting on right now, especially not when I had been suffering in my own purgatory of regret from not giving in and making her mine. Life couldn't possibly be that cruel. But it was, and the universe was showing me that while I got time, she got all the freedom.

Emotionally, I was in pieces, and she had moved on. I was stuck in a permanent place of grieving while she was living the best life possible. How was she able to move forward when she broke my heart? This shit wasn't fair at all.

"Tennyson, is something wrong?"

"No, I just saw someone I used to know," I said, still staring at Isla's pretty ass. It seemed as if life had been better for her than it was to me since she walked out of my office that night. I wanted so badly to go bask in the light that was her, but I just couldn't disturb her peace. In some sick contradictory sense I was elated but mad as hell that she was glowing. I was mad bitter and nothing in this moment was making sense.

She was real deal basking in that post-breakup glow up. I mean, could you really blame her? Isla was bad and everything a nigga knew he needed. I just couldn't get it together to get that from her. As if she felt my eyes on her, she glanced my way and gave a bashful smile before she quickly went back to entertaining her table. She gave me a weak pretty ass smile. How could she not see that I was hurting?

"Tenny you kinda checked out on us there for a minute. Are you sure you're okay?" Rio asked.

"Yeah man, I'm good."

"Aight, well a few of us will be checking out this art exhibit later on this week. If you could stomach being around us a little longer then our workday, we would love for you to come join us."

"I'll see what I can swing." I knew damn well I probably wouldn't be back after I went home and got settled. Lately, it had been the same ole thing with me. I would go home and play my acoustic guitar, until I strummed a melody sweet enough to lead me to bed. Something had to give. God had to give me some direction to get me to a place of happiness. I didn't want to say He owed me this, but I knew after all the hell I'd been through that he would allow a lot of light to crack through this darkness.

The energy radiating between our two anchored souls was enough to make this restaurant explode. There was no way I could continue on without her, but there was no way I could allow myself to be vulnerable with her again. I needed to escape, and fast before I revealed to everyone how weak her love made me. Feeling the room grow smaller, I ran my hand down my beard and excused myself from the table because I had to go. If you've never had to your heart and your brain conflicting, then consider yourself lucky. The shit hurt, so in order to get myself to a place of healing, I knew I had to do one of two things -- run. I didn't think I was up to facing her head on, until I made it out the door and felt her delicate hand grasp my arm.

"Tennyson, can I please have a brief moment of your time?" Isla asked as she scraped her fingers through her hair.

"I'm not sure if this is a good idea or not but follow me next door so that we can have a little bit of privacy," I snarled out unintentionally. I didn't want to be rude to her, but I couldn't go out like a sucker either. I knew, deep down, that one of her kisses would make all my doubts lay dormant. I should've just been honest and worked through our relationship issues way back when. But my pride wouldn't allow me to. There was no way I deserved to be someone's second choice. So I followed my mind.

"Okay. I won't take up too much of your time, Ten," she said while shuffling her feet. I placed my hand on the small of her back and led her into our local coffee shop. As we were greeted with the aroma of espresso beans and warm vanilla, I couldn't help but notice the difference in her demeanor. We ordered a cup of coffee and waited in an uncomfortable silence for our names to be called.

With our coffee in hand, we ventured over to a table near the front of the coffee shop. After pulling her chair out in front of the giant glass windows with a view of the street, I sat myself down in one of the rustic chairs. I took a moment to take her in. Something within her had changed, causing me to see her in an entirely different light, she was no longer the broken woman that left my office six months prior. She seemed lighter, free even, but that could have everything to do with her very public breakup.

Ryder's career seemed to take a hit, especially once everyone got wind of his infidelity with her best friend, nonetheless. Everything would've blown over quietly had he not went to the blogs trying to bash her. The fact that Isla took that hit to the chin with grace and chose not to speak on it at all won America over. In those times, although I was very angry with her, my love grew for her, if that even makes sense.

"The floor is yours, Isla," I said after I took a long sip of my coffee. While I could spend all day getting lost in her beauty it wasn't conducive enough to be sitting here not addressing the elephant in the room. The light she had a little while ago was still shining but I could feel the nervousness of her spirit. She needed to say something and it was only my prayer that whatever it was didn't break me further. There was only so much pain I could take and pour it into my businesses.

"First, thanks for so graciously giving me a little of your time. I know it's been a while, but I honestly appreciate the effort it took to be in this space with me." I nodded to acknowledge her.

"So, how have you been?" she asked while trying to establish eye contact. I was trying to thug it out because I was refusing to let her eyes see what I was so desperately trying to hold on to. My love for her. The pain my heart felt when she walked out the first time and how deep she gutted me the second when I had to turn her away.

"Business has been good, Isla."

"That's not what I asked, love. I didn't ask about your business, the weather, or how the Cubs were playing. I asked about you," she stated while lifting my chin up with her delicate fingers.

My tone was nonchalant, flat even, when I answered her. "I don't know what you expect me to say, doll. We didn't exactly end well. But, to appease you, I will simply state that I've been living."

"Hmmm. Interesting."

"Interesting?" I repeated, raising my eyebrow a bit confused on where this conversation was headed. I didn't put myself through the grief of drinking this coffee and glossing over my pain and giving her small talk.

"Yeah, but I won't dive into that just yet." She took a sip of her coffee and nodded her head before diverting her eyes somewhere else. That gesture made me feel as if she could see right through me and honestly that had me scared. I didn't want her to see that after all this time she still had an effect on me. I didn't want her to see that I was still broken. That she damaged my heart and left me no instructions on how to deal with that trauma.

Isla fidgeted with her hands a bit before she glanced back up at me. "Let me hop right into why I came after you. Tennyson, I'm so sorry that I hurt you. I was so broken, misguided, and lost back then. In my effort to find me, I broke a great man who I'm seeing has never fully recovered from the heartbreak I've caused. I just knew I could love you. I've come to realize that you were me, in male form.

"You came bouncing, literally, into my world with a gorgeous smile and a personality so sweet and so genuine. I'm sure that was my weakness. Like, your soul was *everything*! You held on and reached out in times you had no idea how just hearing your voice or reading a text message would fill me with enough strength to get me through my days. But, still, I pushed you away. I was my own worst enemy when it came to you. I let my own insecurities get in the way and cause me to miss out on something that was potentially great.

"We were great for one another, but my lack of maturity was our downfall. Although I miss us, I can't fault you for not wanting anything to do with me. Just know that the love we shared was real, and it was true. I thank you and hope that one day, you are open to getting all the love I was too selfish to share from someone more deserving. I miss you, King, but I love you enough to release you from this bondage of relationships past."

I sat there completely flummoxed. Everything that I thought I needed to say was stuck in my throat. I never thought I would see the day that Isla showed remorse instead of regret. That's all I needed from her, some sincerity and the will to say, *"Hey I fucked up, and fucked you up in the process."* Hell, if I'm keeping it a buck, I never thought I would fully admit to being broken, but here I was, a thirty-two-year old man, broken and pleading with God to hear my cry. Yet, here I sat with my face in my palms, bawling. There was honestly no words that I could speak that would explain the relief that I was feeling. Was the hurt still there? Of course. But hearing her take ownership of part of my pain was an amazing feeling. It was big of her.

Yeah, people may view this as weak, but I needed this. I tried to be strong for so long that this breakthrough had to happen. The world expected black men to exemplify a strong presence of masculinity, but hell, we got weak too. The world just didn't allow us to show it.

"It's okay, love, let it out," she cooed in my ear as she wrapped her delicate arms around me. "I'm woman enough to offer you the things you need to get to a point of healing. I'm just so sorry it took me so long."

We sat in that embrace for a while. I didn't realize how much I needed that cry until it was pulled from my soul. It seemed for so long, I was searching and running from my own heart coincidentally and simultaneously, at the same time. I couldn't put my finger on it then, but now, I know what I needed to do for me. I needed to forgive her. I found my heart deep down, buried in a broken place, and I knew that in order for me to move on in peace, I needed to have this sit down with her. I had to face the truth instead of reflecting on the love we shared in the past. We were made for each other and destined to be great.

We were each other's forbidden fruit, beautiful enough to hide the toxins we were carrying with other people's shit. She may have thought this was a way to say goodbye, but she had only awakened the beast within. I was going to come for what was mine with a vengeance that rivaled God's love for us. I was gonna get my girl back, come hell or high water. We had so many false starts with not enough gas to make it past the finish line, but damn it this time, we were going to give it one final try.

A couple of days after my run in with Isla I called up a therapist to get down to the source of healing my pain. Yes that apology lifted a lot of dead weight off of my shoulders but it also brought awareness to the fact that I was too code-pendent in our situation. I was so wrapped up in my pain that I was letting life pass me by. I was so hell bent on mourning the lost of that relationship that I got comfortable. Once I got comfortable that blanket of bitterness kept me complacent. I realized being emotionally complacent was blocking blessings that have my name on them, so I had to do something about it. I was going to start the necessary steps to get my girl back but I had to start with me first.

CHAPTER 5

*I*sla

Since having coffee with Tennyson the other week, I felt as if a weight was lifted off my back. I didn't understand the magnitude of the hurt he felt, until I was forced to feel that same hurt. I only halfway loved Ryder's trifling ass and that shit gutted me, so I could only imagine how horrible Tennyson felt. He wanted to pretend he was holding it together, but I saw the hurt behind his eyes.

He could pretend to the world, but I knew his heart. I knew the day that I left his office that he was conflicted with his feelings for me. The damage I did to his heart was clear. I was so used to falling back into his arms as a backup that I failed to realize that I was trying to use the goodness of his heart and love for me to make me whole. I was becoming a narcissist in our love affair. I was taking the things I needed from him and not pouring anything back into him.

It was that realization as well as my heartbreak that allowed me to seek therapy. It was because of therapy that I knew, upon seeing him in that restaurant, that I needed to let him go. It no longer mattered how much I wanted him. I felt his energy and knew what I needed to do for him.

Today was a big day for me, so I needed to get all of my emotions in check. I had been mildly successful with artwork prior to this art gallery commissioning me to do a few pieces for them. It was truly a bittersweet feeling. This was what I had worked my whole life for and, aside from my parents, I had no one to share this moment with. I guess this was what they were hinting at when they said it was lonely at the top. The bright side to that was that I had my peace.

As I made my way into the packed gallery, I said a few hellos to some of the people viewing my pieces. My thoughts were halted as a blast from my recent past made a beeline toward me. One thing I could never stand was people mixing our personal affairs into my business. That shit was beyond tacky. Like, whatever it was could wait until it was convenient for everyone.

"Hey bestie, can we talk?" Jessica asked while rubbing her now budding belly. I swear, it took everything that was good in me not to smack that smug look off her face.

"Bestie?" I asked as I raised my eyebrow.

"Yes, bestie. You can't honestly still be mad, Isla. I gave you your space to adjust to all these changes. But come on, forgive me already. We are better than this."

"I'm not about to do this here. Whatever you think you're about to say will not happen today."

"So, what you're not about to do is dismiss me. That's what you're not gonna do. When else am I supposed to catch you, Isla Maria? You like to play innocent, but we both know you aren't!"

"You know, Jess, the woman I am now feels sorry for you. I am at a place in my life where I forgive you for betraying my trust. But, don't mistake my forgiveness as an invitation back into my life," I declared.

"We've known each other our whole lives, Isla. We can't let what one man did tear us apart. We are better than this, and I miss you, sis. I can't raise this baby without you," she pleaded.

When she uttered the word *baby*, that cut deeper than I wanted it to. It was a reminder that a friendship that I cherished was over. It had nothing to do with Ryder either. It had everything to do with her loyalty and disregard to my feelings.

"If this had everything to do with Ryder, I would welcome you back into my world with open arms. But, this goes deeper than that, Jess. You were my sister. The closest thing to me since I lost my brother; your betrayal cut me deeply. It just wasn't expected. But, what I've come to understand is that I gave you too much of me and equipped you with all the tools you needed to send me free-falling into self-destruction.

"I love you because you've helped me grow, but I don't need you. If you would've asked me a year ago if I foresaw my future without you, I would've cursed you out for even thinking that. But strangely, in this moment today, I'm okay with it. In fact, I'm welcoming this journey with open arms. Your type of love is toxic. I don't need it. I've been my best self without you, so as much as it pains me, I had to end the saga of you. I wish you the best of luck on your journey. If you would excuse me, I see some investors I need to greet. Please, stay and enjoy the party."

"You can't do this to me. If you were with Tennyson, you would be okay with the past Ryder and I shared. Was it wrong for me to fall for him? Yes, but you opened the door for that. You ignored us once you got a little bit of fame from this art shit. We just happened, and it didn't help that I knew the majority of your paintings were telling the story of you and Ten! You made this happen, so you don't get to walk out of my life like I'm some monster when you're just like me!" she cried out.

I glared at her for a moment, to take in what she said. Everything she said was false and definitely coming from a hurt place. Everything but what was the inspiration behind my paintings, that is. My muse was the life I shared with Tennyson, and my angry portion was the turmoil I felt being with Ryder. Was it wrong? Probably, but who said that art had to be right? No one.

Furthermore, how could the two people I loved more than I loved myself at that point think it was okay to do something like that to me? Her logic was baffling. But, I guess hurt people did strange things to make you feel what they were feeling. Unfortunately for her, I had already been in this hurt and pulled myself out. Regardless of whether Ryder was going to be in her life or not, my black ass would never be.

"I'm going to let you have your moment right now, because I know everything that's coming out of your mouth is coming from a hurt place. Once that moment is over, I need you to leave. A temper tantrum at thirty-one is unbecoming of a woman. I don't bend or move to guilt trips, you know that. Again, I wish you well on your journey," I declared as I patted her on her shoulder and walked off.

I found no reason to sit here and argue with her. Most people stayed around pondering and beating a dead horse about things that no longer served them a purpose. If you were truly done with a situation and felt an overall peace about it, nothing would move you. It wasn't you being cold;

it was just you accepting the time in the sun you both had and making the conscious choice in moving on.

I could acknowledge your hurt without you making me feel bad for it. There was no reason to make a person feel bad for their feelings, because they were valid. A person had a right to feel however they would like without you making them feel bad about it. Therapy provided that knowledge for me, because there was no way I would have been receptive to any of this a few months back.

Feeling as if someone was watching me, I took a quick glance around the room and saw Tennyson looking at me, as if I was the last slice of German chocolate cake. It took me a moment to catch my breath; his gaze was so strong that for a moment, I forgot that there were other people in the building besides the two of us. When he licked his lips, I felt my soul drop out of my panties. I honestly didn't know how to feel seeing him.

The devil was surely busy because this had to be his work. If Ryder showed his ass up, I would die. The universe knew there was only so much I could take in a day. Choosing to ignore the desire I saw in his eyes, I went straight over to the art gallery's manager. I had things to do, and I would not lose focus worrying about anything other than my art. I'd done that before and look where it got me, sad, depressed and alone. I took ownership of the hurt that I left him with and hopefully left him with a clean conscience.

The only thing he had ever done for me was love me without flaws and I walked away from that like an idiot. Ryder had all the money in the world but he still couldn't provide me with the basic things I knew I needed for survival. All I needed was a sense of peace and a love that provided stability. Oh to be young and truly dumb. If I could go back in time I would ride the trenches with Tennyson and build not only my brand up but me as well.

When you are broken and desperate for a breakthrough you would do almost anything to get to a space of completion. Not realizing that being satisfied with the blessings you have would get you to the place you needed to be much faster than jumping into the next greatest thing. How often do we forget that the devil himself delivered blessings disguised as gifts? Never again would I make that same mistake twice.

So while I wanted Ten, I wasn't about to go down that road with whatever he was thinking. He needed to heal and I mean truly heal before I would even open that door back up to him. I needed him to work out the kinks in his life before I started to pursue him.

"This is beautiful Isla. What was the inspiration behind this piece?"

I looked over to where Tennyson was holding a conversation with a group of our peers and then back to the canvas of a beautifully broken man before I spoke. It took me a minute to find the words but once I did it fit perfectly.

"A love unfulfilled."

"Do you hear that Jilly? You should buy this for Emerson." The owner of my favorite restaurant Soulatarian giggled out.

"Girl shut up. You barely secured your own love so don't go telling me how to get a man I have no interest in. The nerve of some folk," Jillian seethed before she took a sip of her wine.

"I'm only stating the obvious. I'm not the only one that notices the chemistry between the two of you. Learn from me and my mistakes before it's too late," Olivia stated, clearly offended with her friend

"Liv, no need to push her. We all move in our own timing. It's best that she moves in accordance with her spirit otherwise she stands to miss out on something beautiful. If you ladies would excuse me I need to go and check on a few more guests. Please enjoy yourself."

I excused myself to go take a breather. After the encounter with Jessica, seeing Tennyson in my space, and hearing their banter I needed to meditate before I could put on a brave face and greet the crowd.

CHAPTER 6

*T*ennyson

Walking through this gallery had me taken aback. Isla was gifted. She wove a beautiful story of our love without revealing too much. Everything I dreamed about our love was laid out before me in the form of fine art. It was sensual, but not overtly sexual. She showed me her heart, and I was taken aback. I'd never seen the woman so vulnerable and transparent with her feelings. It honestly made me love her so much more.

I wanted to approach her to tell her how proud I was of her but seeing her trash ass best friend storm out of the gallery holding her small round belly, I took the coward way out and continued to peep her artwork. I was stunned into silence as I stood before a portrait of her. The piece itself was titled *Naked*.

She was submerged in water, sprinkled with sunflowers and roses in a bear clawed tub. She was staring directly into the camera. There, I saw her soul. I saw what she was so desperately trying to hide from the world. The portrait showed the conflict she had within herself. She tried her hardest to mask her pain outside of this painting, but as with all things Isla, this started to pour out into her artwork. I searched the room, until my gaze fell upon her. She quickly averted her eyes and began to make conversation with a group of people, forcing herself to not look at me.

"This piece is interesting," I heard a woman next to me state. "The bold colors against the grey of the woman's skin is telling the tale of a confused soul. You can sense the turmoil behind the unshed tears we see in her eyes. It has to be awful not being able to live life boldly. Although it's sad, I love it."

I was completely shocked; like damn, someone other than me gets it. They get her. They saw the her that was hidden from the world. I realized then that Isla and I weren't as different as we thought. We were made for one another, and it was high time that we acknowledged it and stopped playing.

"Yo, Ten, man, I see the look in your eyes. Whatever you're thinking about doing, let it go. I brought you here so that you would stop feeling guilty and mourning the remnants of a love lost. Don't ruin this woman's night trying to fix your own heart," Rio stated while placing his hand on my shoulder. I waved him off. I wasn't trying to hear what he was trying to say.

I got what he was trying to do, but what he was implying couldn't be further from the truth. I didn't want to ruin her night; hell, even on her night, I only wanted to make it better. I spent so much time hurting and being mad at her, that it took so much time away from us coming together and appreciating what God blessed us with. Our love was the cure to all of the bad that tore down our happiness. I was going to make this right. As the speaker was getting everyone's attention, I knew it was now or never to get what I needed to say out.

I grabbed the mic out of his hands and said, "Good evening, everyone. My name is Tennyson Hampton, and I would like to say a few words about our guest of honor."

She stood there silent, mentally pleading with me to step away from the mic and not say anything that would show her in a bad light. I watched her freak out internally and bite her lips to hide her growing frustration with me, but now that I had the floor, nothing was going to stop me.

"Ten years ago, I met this beautiful, brown-skinned woman in an art store. I tried my hardest to resist the urge to talk to her, but her laugh was so infectious that I approached her. Now, anyone that knows Isla knows she has never met a stranger, but this day, she was stunned into silence.

When asked why she was so quiet, she responded, *"When God places perfection at your feet, you take your time to appreciate it. If you're lucky, you get to hold on to that prize. If not, you duplicate it; that's the beauty of the world."*

I saw a faint smile appear on her face, so I knew she was warming up and becoming receptive to all that I needed to say.

"You see, I never quite understood what she meant until I watched her waste her time on a generic copy of me. The funny thing about life is while we are waiting on the sidelines, longing for the green grass in someone else's yard, God's busy preparing your feast. I stood by and watched this woman neglect her own yard in search of paradise I felt she already had in me. I tried so hard to fight it, but God himself brought me healing in the form of you, Isla Maria Danielson, and I was wondering if you would consider watering your own grass and doing life with me for real this time?"

As if no one in the room was there, my girl came running to me with tears running down her face. But I couldn't read her. I couldn't get a handle on what she was truly feeling. I knew she loved me but had too much time passed? Could we come back from this?

"There is nothing I want more in this world than to water my own grass and spend the next eternity loving you. But can we first start with a date and reconnecting first?"

"I wouldn't have it any other way," I said as I pulled her in for a sweet kiss.

*I*sla

After my event things with Tennyson and I blossomed. These last couple of weeks had to have been some of the toughest, most vulnerable, challenging, loving times of our lives. But we got through it. We survived and grew deeply in love. That probably had something to do with us coming back into this relationship with a plan.

Our first date was to the therapist office where we were able to address what tore us apart in the first place. I was able to help him understand that it wasn't him I was running from. I had past trauma that didn't include him but it did directly affect him. I required stability and at any moment that I didn't feel stable I fled the scene.

Once I realized how toxic it was, I addressed it and made it my point to be vocal on my likes and dislikes. Tennyson also made it a point to set clear boundaries that I couldn't cross.

We both knew we were lucky to get a second chance at this love because there wouldn't be a third. This was it. So we worked hard at perfecting the love we had. I looked up at the night sky and thought back on the many nights I wished I had him back in my life. I closed my eyes for a moment silently thanking the universe for reconnecting us. When I opened my eyes he was staring back at me. I saw love. I saw peace. And if I'm being honest I also saw my forever.

"Are you ready to head out?"

"About as ready as I'm gonna be. Where are we headed?" Tennyson asked as he slid his feet into his favorite pair of Chelsea boots.

I took a moment to admire him. His aura was no longer dark. It had this beautiful glow around him. He seemed to be at peace and just overall in a positive space. I couldn't just credit us getting back together for this new person I saw in him. No, this was a result of him putting in the work just as I did to heal the gaps in his soul. Him doing that magnified the love we had for each other. It allowed us to compliment each other without being codependent.

"That is classified information sir. Just sit back and enjoy the ride"

When he didn't put up a fight I winked and headed to the car. The ride was mostly silent with the exception of Anthony Hamilton serenading us.

We rode for a bit before we pulled up to a rustic building. We were right in the heart of downtown directly across the street from where we first met. The bewildered look on his face made me chuckle. He was never one to like being surprised with anything. But dealing with me it was something he had to learn to expect. After opening my door and helping me out we stood just staring at the building with the beautiful green bow on the door.

"Care to explain what we're looking at Isla?"

"Your restaurant."

"My restaurant?"

"Yes, your restaurant. These were all of your ideas. I only brought them to life."

"Thank you. How? I mean why?" he stuttered out.

"For so long you've extended your heart to me during times that I was really undeserving of you and your love. You dealt with the broken parts of me and neglected some of the things you wanted most. Many moons ago you wrote down a plan in a journal I'm sure you may have forgotten. Although you're pretty successful on the nightlife scene you wanted something that we could pass down and establish generational wealth and love with. Even if we didn't end up together I was going to find a way to gift this to you."

"What are you saying Doll? What is all of this?" Tennyson asked, still not grasping what was happening.

"I'm saying that I combined our interest, fine dining, Art, love, wine and spirits and birthed our first baby. I present to you Green Pastures! I didn't do any decorating aside from the pieces of art that mean the most to you. Do as you please with this restaurant. I can't wait to see what you come up with."

"Doll, I'm speechless. How long have you been planning this?"

"Since the night you stood your ground and didn't allow the broken side of me to come in and damage your heart more."

He suddenly picked me up and spun me around smiling and showering me with kisses. With each kiss I could feel his love and appreciation for me. I could feel the happiness radiating off of him. I couldn't help but think had I been patient I wouldn't have lost so much time loving him. But those thoughts were quickly halted when I realized without getting the individual and joint healing we needed we would've fumbled this love and gotten to a place we couldn't return from.

I had to experience the heartache of losing him before I could truly appreciate the love that I found here on greener pastures. Now that I had it, I was going to do everything in my power to nurture and grow this love.

AFTERWORD

Want to connect with me? You can reach me here:

Website:

www.brittjonipens.com

Hippie•ish

www.brittjonipens.com/hippieish

Like page:

http://bit.ly/likeBrittJoni

Group:

http://bit.ly/booksnsoulwork

I'm also on Instagram & Twitter: @authorbrittjoni

CPSIA information can be obtained
at www.ICGtesting.com
Printed in the USA
LVHW092042061120
670968LV00007B/1227